SEASONS WITH

FISHMONGER

AND

WORDSMITH

Seasons with

Fishmonger

and

Wordsmith

FRIENDSHIP STORIES

Kristina Drake

First paperback edition January 2024

Book design by Kristina Drake
Illustrations by Kristina Drake

ISBN 978-1-7382211-1-0

Published by Cat Creek
www.kristinadrake.ca

For FC—

I carry your friendship with me

everywhere, always

Essential

Wordsmith looked out the window at the bright, melty spring day. A family of black squirrels ran along the cedar-rail fence and up the trunk of a large spruce. Up and down, up and down, they scampered. The breeze came in through the open window and was fresh with sunshine and a promising warmth. There seemed to be an energy making everything vibrate and grow.

Wordsmith, though, felt glum. She looked outside at the day—and the squirrels and the sunshine and the green—and felt dejected, tired, and alone. She thought about the busy squirrels. She thought about the birds, and the sunshine. She thought how all these things needed each other, perfectly. The grass, the worms, the nuts and pine cones. Outside was full of life. Wordsmith did not feel full of life.

She wanted to sleep, but it was the middle of the day. Sleeping in the middle of the day is a nap, and Wordsmith did not take naps. She thought they were unproductive. But today, she was an untired sort of tired. She was too tired even to decide to nap. She thought, "What is wrong with me?"

Wordsmith looked around her room, and at the things on the shelves. Usually, these books and pictures and bits and pieces seemed beautiful to her. Today, they seemed covered in dust. Why did she keep so many useless things? She did not need

them. She almost never used them. All they did, all day long, was collect dust. She felt like she was collecting dust, too.

The breeze made the curtain flutter. Wordsmith thought, "I know, I should start tidying! Get rid of some of this clutter!" But she didn't move from her chair. She watched the squirrels some more. They were so active! So busy! What would it be like to be a squirrel in a family of squirrels? Wordsmith rested her head back against the chair to ponder that thought.

From the distance, there was a noise. It sounded like cheering. Clapping? "What could be happening?" wondered Wordsmith.

Wordsmith peered out the window to get a glimpse of the road. Several cars were driving slowly

by. A few people walked alongside the cars carrying signs. Wordsmith wondered what was going on. The people weren't supposed to leave their homes. The government said there was a bad sickness, and everyone needed to stay home. That's why Wordsmith was sitting  at her window feeling glum. Why were these other people

outside walking and cheering?

Wordsmith went to her front door for a better view. What a strange procession!

"THANK YOU, ESSENTIAL WORKERS!"

"BRAVO, NURSES & DOCTORS!"

"WE COUNT ON YOU!"

Wordsmith watched until the last car had passed. She closed the door quietly. It's true, she thought. We need the doctors and nurses to beat this terrible sickness. They're essential. If I get sick, I'll need them. But I'd rather not get sick, so I'll stay home. Wordsmith went back to the window, and the squirrels, and her tired thoughts.

She watched the squirrels. The squirrels didn't know she was there. Would it help them if she put out some food? No, that was silly. Squirrels don't need people to feed them. Besides, she wasn't a squirrel feeder. She was a wordsmith.

Did anyone need her words? No. Everyone had words of their own. Most people didn't even care about words. What wordsmiths did with words was not essential.

She wondered who would need her. The thought came slowly and quietly. Wordsmith almost didn't notice it appearing. But there it was. She rolled it around in her mind a little bit before really thinking it: No one needed her.

Wordsmith looked at her room of dusty things. She didn't need these things. She didn't do anything important with any of it. In fact, she didn't do anything important at all. Wordsmith was not essential.

Wordsmith felt empty. She felt dusty. And cold, and tired, and unessential. She wished she were asleep. Unproductive napping was better than being unessential. This *unessential* thought was an unhappy thought. But now that she had thought it, it would not go away.

Wordsmith thought about the meaning of *essential*. What was essential to her? Words were essential. She couldn't be a wordsmith without them. What else? Food, water, oxygen, yes. These were more than essential.

At that moment, there was a knock, a gleeful sounding knock, at the door.

Fishmonger was standing on the front step with a package in her arms. Fishmonger was smiling, and seeing her made Wordsmith

very happy. She felt her mood lift and a smile grow across her face. Fishmonger was here! Suddenly, Wordsmith realized how much she had been missing her good friend. Fishmonger was just exactly who she needed to see.

Fishmonger put the package down. It contained smoked fish and cheese, treats from the market. But the real treat was to see Fishmonger. Wordsmith welcomed her friend inside and rushed to put on the coffee. The sun seemed suddenly brighter. Wordsmith no longer noticed the dust suspended in the rays of sunlight. She saw her friend, and she was happy.

Wordsmith poured the coffee into two cups and told Fishmonger about the cheering people who had passed by. She said, "The nurses and doctors help people, and that's good. It's good that they are appreciated."

Wordsmith remembered how she had felt alone and tired. "But, Fishmonger, I was feeling sad and lonely before you arrived, and seeing you made me happy. You are essential to me. I'm so glad you're my friend."

The two friends sipped the hot coffee and enjoyed the peaceful warmth of the afternoon sun and the possibilities of spring in the air.

The Suitcase

Wordsmith looked around her room. It was morning. Through the window, she saw the bare trees. They waved their branches lightly in the wind. The sky was grey and the winter clouds shivered in the cold. Winter was coming.

Wordsmith sat down on her bed in her cozy room and sighed. She liked her room. She liked the dark wood floor. She liked her things on the shelves around her. She liked her quilted blanket and the way the sunrise came in the room. She felt warm.

Wordsmith held a list in her hand. It was written on a page she had torn out of her notebook.

It said:

- Quilted work jacket
- Deodorant

- Brown sugar
- Maple syrup
- Tablecloths

A large black suitcase was open on the other side of the bed. It was unzipped and lay flat open like a hardcover book. Like a crocodile mouth. Like a clam.

Wordsmith thought about all the things the suitcase could be compared to. Things that opened and closed, that chomped and clamped shut. She eyeballed it warily. It was already almost full.

Wordsmith sighed at the suitcase. It was big and heavy and full, and soon she would need to close it up and take it downstairs.

She looked back out the window at the bare, waving trees. The view from her window was prettier and bigger than the suitcase.

"Fishmonger," Wordsmith said, "I'm going away for a while."

"I know," said Fishmonger. "You're going on a great adventure."

"Yes," said Wordsmith. "I'm going on a great adventure." She scratched her knee. "Why don't I feel like I'm going on an adventure?"

"I don't know," said Fishmonger. "Have you asked yourself? That's what I do when I'm not sure of something."

Wordsmith was silent. She was trying to ask herself, but she wasn't sure how to go about it.

"Anyway, *I* know for sure that you are going on an adventure. A *very* great adventure." Quietly, Fishmonger said, "I wish I could go with you."

"I wish you could come with me, too," said Wordsmith. "But the fish and the animals need you.

I need you a lot, but they need you more."

The two friends thought about Fishmonger's farm—the pigs, the sheep, the chickens and ducks and geese, and the dogs and cats. Who would feed them if Fishmonger weren't there?

"Fishmonger," Wordsmith continued, "do you ever wish you weren't home?"

"Yes, sometimes," said Fishmonger. "Sometimes, I wish I was in my boat."

"And what do you do then?"

"Well, I go out on the river in my boat."

"And then you're happy?"

"No. Then, I remember how warm it is at home, and I wish I was at home."

"And what do you do then?"

"I go home. And sometimes I drink hot cocoa and eat cake."

Fishmonger and Wordsmith looked at their plates and the crumbs. They looked at the cake pan and then they thought about the wise and unwise things they might do.

Most of the cake was already gone. They had each had a couple of slices. They knew from experience that finishing it would be a bad idea.

"Do you ever wish you could go somewhere far away?" asked Wordsmith.

"Oh," said Fishmonger. "Yes, of course I do. Sometimes I wish I could be in a country where there are white sandy beaches or big mountains."

"Me too," said Wordsmith. "But I don't

like having to pack my suitcase. I can't take the important things with me. They don't fit."

"Right now, I wish I was in your suitcase," said Fishmonger.

"Me too," said Wordsmith.

"Wordsmith?" Fishmonger knocked on Wordsmith's door. "Are you there?"

"No." Came a voice that sounded a lot like Wordsmith's voice. "I don't know where I am."

"Well, I can hear you," said Fishmonger. "You must be there."

"I'm not so sure," said Wordsmith. "I might be somewhere else."

Fishmonger pushed the door open wider.

"Wordsmith, I can see you. You're right here in front of me."

"Oh, good! Thank you, Fishmonger. I was getting worried."

"But you look sad, Wordsmith. Are you sad?"

"I don't know that, either, Fishmonger. If I look sad, maybe I am sad?"

Fishmonger sat down on the bed beside Wordsmith. There wasn't much space, but Wordsmith scootched over closer to her suitcase.

"What are you doing?" asked Fishmonger, looking at the overflowing black suitcase.

"I'm going away," said Wordsmith. "Again."

"I know," said Fishmonger. "You're going on an another adventure."

"I think I'm lost," said Wordsmith. "I don't know where home is anymore."

"Don't be silly. Your home is here. It will be right here when you come back. And I'll be here too, waiting for you."

"Fishmonger, what if I get lost and I forget how to find home? Will you come find me?"

"Of course I will."

"Oh, good. I was worried about that too. I won't be lost if you'll come find me.

"Now, will you sit on this suitcase for me so I can close it? I didn't pack everything I wanted to, and it is already too full."

"You're quite silly," said Fishmonger, climbing onto the black suitcase and giving it a bounce to squish down the contents. "Are you sure there's no room in there for me?"

Fishmonger put all her weight into keeping the two halves together while Wordsmith zipped them closed and clasped the straps.

Wordsmith thought woefully about all the things she would miss and all the things she couldn't bring with her. And just as she was about to feel sad again, she thought of something else: something she could bring, something that would fit in the very full suitcase. It wouldn't take any room at all!

She could bring stories. And memories and love and joy and laughter.

Wordsmith suddenly felt so much better. She wouldn't get lost! She would have exactly the things she needed to find her way home, where Fishmonger would be waiting for her with all her animals.

Wordsmith thought her suitcase was exactly like a book. It had a front and a back and a bunch of important and not-so-important stuff in the middle. Some days it would be hard to close, but it would never be too full for the really important stuff.

It might even be just a little bit like having home with her, wherever she went.

Christmas Lights

The lights from the Christmas tree twinkled and sparkled red, green, yellow, and blue. The angel on the top of the tree looked down, wise and kind and benevolent, at Fishmonger and Wordsmith.

The two friends were decorated in the colours from the Christmas tree lights. They felt just as sparkly as the tree. They each held a mug of steaming hot chocolate in their hands. The hot chocolate had whipped cream and small, colourful marshmallows on top because today was a special day.

Today was Christmas.

Under the tree were two presents. One of them was wrapped in brown paper. It had a big fish drawn on it and a small red bow. That one was for Fishmonger. The other present was wrapped in blue paper that shimmered like the surface of a lake on a sunny day. That one was for Wordsmith.

The lights of the Christmas tree danced on the presents. Fishmonger and Wordsmith held their hot chocolates and looked at their presents. The angel looked down on everything: the lights, the presents, the hot chocolates, and the two friends.

"Fishmonger," said Wordsmith, "isn't the hot chocolate tasty?"

"Yes, the hot chocolate is tasty," said Fishmonger. "Aren't the presents pretty?"

"Yes, the presents are pretty," said Wordsmith. "The tree is beautiful, too."

"And the lights."

"Yes, and the lights."

"Wordsmith," said Fishmonger, "we are lucky to have Christmas, aren't we?"

"Yes, I think so," said Wordsmith. "What do you like best about Christmas, Fishmonger?"

Fishmonger took a sip of her hot chocolate. She was thinking. There were many things to like about Christmas, and she was thinking about each one of them.

"I like the dancing lights on the snow. What do you like best, Wordsmith?"

"I like the beautiful angels watching over us."

Wordsmith felt very calm and her heart was happy. There weren't many words moving around in her head, just a few: Love, Peace, Warmth.

"Do you feel happy?" asked Wordsmith.

"Yes, I do," said Fishmonger.

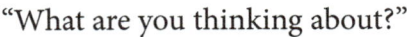

"What are you thinking about?"

"I'm thinking about the fish sleeping in the lake under the ice. I hope they are as cozy as we are."

"Do you think they have hot chocolate, too?"

Fishmonger laughed and then giggled.

"You're quite silly, Wordsmith. Fish don't drink hot chocolate."

"I know, Fishmonger, but I like the idea of it. The idea made me smile, and it made you laugh."

The two friends sipped their hot chocolate. The small, colourful marshmallows had become soft, and left streaks of pink, green, and yellow in the melted whipped cream. It was like drinking Christmas tree lights. It was delicious.

"Fishmonger," said Wordsmith, "should we open our presents now?"

"We could," said Fishmonger, "but let's not. Let's wait a little longer."

The two friends sat in silence.

In the silence, another word came into Wordsmith's mind: Grateful.

She was very, very grateful to have a friend like Fishmonger.

"Fishmonger?"

"Yes?"

"You know what I like best about Christmas?"

"The angels?"

"No, I've changed my mind. What I like best about Christmas is sitting here with you."

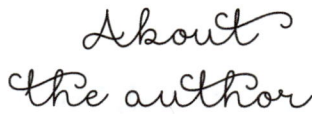

About the author

Kristina Drake is an author, poet and editor living and writing off the beaten path in Canada and Hungary.

Her chapbook *Ornithologies* was published by above/ground press in 2017, and her poems have appeared in *Carte Blanche* and *Soliloquies*.

www.kristinadrake.ca

Cat
Creek

Fishmonger and Wordsmith is a

Cat Creek publication.

More Stories

Enjoy more friendship stories and adventures

with Fishmonger and Wordsmith!

Fishmonger and Wordsmith